Spooktacular!

Don't miss any of the haunted

adventures at Boo La La!

#1: School for Ghost Girls

#2: Spooktacular!

Spooktacular!

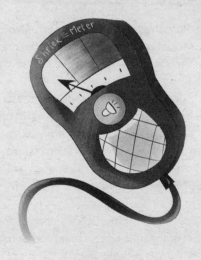

By Rebecca Gómez

SCHOLASTIC INC.

This one's for the boys:
Leonardo, Felipe, Mateo, and Rubén

Text copyright © 2016 by Rebecca Gómez
Illustrations copyright © 2016 by Scholastic Inc.

ISBN 978-0-545-91799-5

10 9 8 7 6 5 4 3 2 1   16 17 18 19 20

Printed in the U.S.A.   40
First printing, September 2016
Book design by Lizzy Yoder

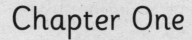

Chapter One

The autumn sun was sinking low in the sky when the shrieking began. Long, loud, eerie wails echoed in the gathering darkness.

Aaaaaiiieeeee! Aaaaaiiieeeee!

Across the spacious grounds of Boo Academy—affectionately known as Boo La La—rabbits and squirrels scurried to safety, frightened by the noise. Boo Academy might be the nation's premiere haunting school, but that didn't make the noises any less scary!

Inside a top-floor classroom in Coffin Hall, twelve third-grade ghost girls stood in a neat line. Best friends Maude, Tiny, and CJ smiled at one another. Mr. Clank, their Intermediate Haunting teacher, sat in front of them, holding a microphone attached to a meter. "Come on, girls, you can do better than that!" he urged.

The girls let out another round of shrieks, but Mr. Clank didn't look satisfied.

"Those sounded more like moans than shrieks," he chided. "I know it's the end of the day and you're all tired, but the NOGS shrieking test is fast approaching!"

The National Organization of Ghost Schools, or NOGS, tested all ghost students in certain grades each year. Third graders were tested on shrieking.

"Can't we just practice more tomorrow?" Lucinda asked in a cranky voice. Shrieking was not her best subject.

"Oh, you *will* be practicing," Mr. Clank assured her. "But as your Haunting teacher, it's my job to get you ready to pass the exam." He turned to Maude and said, "Maude, can you demonstrate?"

"Sure, Mr. Clank," Maude cheerfully agreed from her spot in the middle of the line, sandwiched between Tiny and CJ. After all, as one of Boo Academy's top students, Maude was used to being called on in class. In fact, she loved being called on! And with shrieking talent like hers, she felt she had almost an obligation to help the other ghost girls.

Maude stepped confidently forward and took a deep breath. Then she opened her mouth and released a shriek so loud and piercing that the classroom windows rattled. The dial on Mr. Clank's meter swung wildly.

"Now *that's* a shriek!" he said when everyone's ears stopped ringing. "Did you see the dial? The needle swung all the way into the gray zone. Each of you will be required to produce a grayzone shriek when you go before the NOGS officials."

"Why is this such a big deal?" Helen whined.

She was Lucinda's sidekick, and always agreed with her.

"Why?" Mr. Clank asked, incredulously. He looked around at his students. "Who can explain to Helen why good shrieking technique is so vital?"

"It helps us haunt better," Tiny offered.

"Yes," said Mr. Clank. "But how?"

"Any ghost worth a bag of bones should have a good shriek," Lucinda explained, with a sigh. "Shrieking is our trademark."

"And sometimes, chain rattling, moaning, or flickering lights are simply not enough to get the attention of humans," Maude added.

"Exactly!" Mr. Clank cried, delighted. "We ghosts must have a whole repertoire of tricks for our visitations with humans. A good, solid shriek is as important as passing through walls."

Maude shot CJ a knowing look and gave her arm a small squeeze.

"Let's take a few minutes so that each of you can practice." Mr. Clank said, and turned off his meter.

With that, the room was filled with the noises of twelve wailing girl ghosts.

Aaaaaiiieeeee! Aaaaaiiieeeee! Peep!

Aaaaaiiieeeee! Aaaaaiiieeeee! Peep!

"Silence, everyone!" Mr. Clank said. He looked

around with a puzzled expression. "Who's making that peeping noise?"

The girls looked at one another uneasily.

"It's CJ, Mr. Clank," Lucinda announced in a sly voice.

Maude sighed. Lucinda never missed a chance to point out someone else doing something incorrectly. Of course, she never seemed to realize when *she* was in the wrong!

"Why are you peeping instead of shrieking, CJ?" Mr. Clank asked kindly.

CJ shrugged her shoulders nervously. She could feel her face turning red. That made her even more embarrassed, because a pale ghost with a bright red face is a very strange sight. Maude and Tiny inched closer to her.

"I'm sorry, Mr. Clank," CJ stammered. "I'm not trying to peep. I'm just not a very strong shrieker. I mean, I did the shrieking exercises all summer and I practiced a lot. I'm not sure why I can't do it. I *want* to be a good shrieker. My parents are good shriekers, and my brother—*ouch!*"

CJ stopped talking when Maude gave her a gentle pinch. Her friends knew that when CJ got nervous, she couldn't stop talking. Sometimes they had to help her.

"You do know that you must pass your NOGS shrieking test?" Mr. Clank asked.

"Yes," CJ answered.

"And you know that it's less than a month away?" Mr. Clank continued.

"Yes," CJ gulped.

"Mr. Clank!" Lucinda raised her hand, but immediately started speaking. "Isn't it true that if a student is unable to pass the NOGS test, she will be asked to leave Boo Academy?"

"Well, yes," Mr. Clank answered. "Strictly speaking, that is true, but—"

"It's understandable," Lucinda interrupted. She turned to look at her fellow third-grade ghosts. "After all, Boo Academy could not call itself the best haunting school in the nation if it didn't train first-class ghosts."

"You are correct, Lucinda." Mr. Clank continued. "But—"

Gong! Gong! Gong!

The gong signaling the end of class interrupted him. "Time for dinner," Mr. Clank said. "We'll pick up here the day after tomorrow. Please, girls, try to fit in some practice time between now and then."

As the girls floated out of the room, Mr. Clank pulled CJ aside. "Don't be too nervous," he said. "You've still got time to work on that shriek."

CJ nodded glumly, then caught up with her friends. As she did, Lucinda came up to her, with Helen trailing close behind.

"You'd better practice, CJ," she warned. "If you're not shriek proficient, you're out the door!"

"Stop being mean, Lucinda!" Tiny said. "CJ is good at lots of things. She draws really well and, as you know, she's an absolute master of levitation." CJ had outscored Lucinda on an important levitation exam the previous year.

"I'm not being mean," Lucinda declared angrily. "Rules are rules. CJ has to pass the shrieking test. We all do. The reputation of Boo Academy depends on it." She and Helen pushed past toward the dining hall.

"Don't worry," Maude assured CJ and Tiny. "I'm Boo La La's best shrieker and I'm going to make sure CJ passes with flying colors!"

"I hope you're right!" CJ said.

"I usually am," Maude said loftily.

CJ and Tiny rolled their eyes and smiled, but they couldn't disagree. It was true.

Holding their trays of food, the three friends found seats together in the dining room. It was a huge space, but cozy—it had old, moldy wood-paneled walls covered with hanging cobwebs.

"I love Cook Eerie's meatloaf!" Tiny said, sighing happily as she took a heaping mouthful. Her tray was overloaded with meatloaf, green beans, potatoes, chocolate milk, bananas, and ice cream.

"You love everything Cook Eerie makes," Maude teased her.

"It's true!" Tiny grinned. "It's not easy keeping my basketball player–sized tummy filled!"

"Hello, girls!" a cheery voice boomed. It was Ms. Finley, their dorm mother, passing them on her way to the faculty table.

"Hello, Ms. Finley," the third-grade ghosts answered in unison.

Maude leaned in to her friends and whispered, "I'm just glad we proved, once and for all, that Ms. Finley is one hundred percent ghost!"

"I still can't believe we ever thought she was . . . *human!*" Tiny said with a shiver.

They all looked down at the brown lace-up oxfords peeking out from under Ms. Finley's long skirt. As a rule, ghosts never wear shoes, but the girls had gotten used to seeing Ms. Finley's. They knew now that her shoes were prescribed by a doctor and that she took them off while haunting.

The girls then looked at Ms. Finley's glasses. This evening, they were shiny pink frames with small black spiders printed on them. She seemed to have a different pair every day!

"I'm so glad Ms. Finley came back to Boo Academy." CJ sighed.

"You know what they say," Maude agreed, "Once a Boo girl, always a Boo girl!"

"Boo La La!" the three friends chanted quietly, laughing while they ate.

As dinner wound down, Principal Von Howl stood at the head of the faculty table and clapped his hands. "Attention, ladies!" he called, and the dining room slowly quieted.

"Not too many announcements tonight," he began, "but I did want to talk about the NOGS testing coming up in less than a month for grades three, six, nine, and twelve."

The students all groaned. They'd already started hearing about the testing in their classes!

Principal Von Howl ignored their groans and continued, "As a reminder, twelfth graders are tested on levitation, ninth graders are tested on emanations and auras, sixth graders are tested on passing through, and third graders are tested on shrieking."

CJ looked nervously at the faces of the ghost girls around her.

The principal continued, "It is my duty to remind you that failure to pass the grade-appropriate national test has very serious consequences. However, I have no doubt that each and every one of you will pass with flying colors. After all, you wouldn't have been admitted to Boo Academy if we

didn't think you had potential!" The hall filled with whispers as his speech wrapped up.

As Maude, CJ, and Tiny cleared their places, Ms. Finley bustled over.

"I almost forgot, Maude," she puffed. "While I was in the library today doing some research on my Venus flytrap collection, I had such a lovely conversation with Mrs. Guttenberg about all sorts of dangerous plants. She is extremely knowledge-able. They don't call her Nightshade Guttenberg for nothing!" Ms. Finley shook with laughter, and Maude smiled politely.

Her chuckles subsided. "Anyway, she asked me to give you this," she said, and handed Maude a folded slip of paper.

"What does the librarian want with you, Maude?" CJ asked.

"She probably has a bunch of overdue books," Lucinda sniped as she floated by.

Maude rolled her eyes at Lucinda, but then confessed to CJ and Tiny, "I don't know what she wants. Let's go somewhere more private and I'll read her note!"

Chapter Two

"What does it say?" Tiny asked as Maude unfolded the sheet of paper.

The girls were sprawled on Maude's bed in their shared dorm room. They'd been careful to close the door behind them—they wouldn't put it past Lucinda to hover outside, hoping to hear something about the mysterious note. She seemed to live for the chance to get the three of them in trouble.

"Dear Maude," Maude began to read aloud, "I've noticed that you come to the library quite frequently. I very much enjoy our informal book discussions. As you know, there's nothing I like to see more than my students reading! Would you be interested in volunteering at the library? We could arrange a few shifts per week, working around your class schedule, of course. Please see me at your convenience. Best regards, Mrs. Guttenberg."

"Ugh!" Tiny said. "That sounds awful!"

"No it doesn't," Maude disagreed. She liked the library a lot. "I think it sounds like fun!"

"Remember, Tiny," CJ said, mimicking Principal Von Howl's deep voice, "one ghost's strange is another ghost's normal!"

The friends were still laughing when there were three knocks on their door. Polite ghost custom was to knock three times before entering a room where other ghosts were gathered.

It was Ms. Finley. "What's all the noise?" she grumbled playfully.

"I'm so excited, Ms. Finley!" Maude answered. "Mrs. Guttenberg has asked me to be a library volunteer!"

"Why, that's wonderful," Ms. Finley answered. "It's quite an honor. I know how much you enjoy books. It's the perfect job for you!"

"Just don't get carried away, Maude," Tiny warned. "I'm not sure our room can hold many more books!"

"Oops! Sorry!" Maude giggled. She looked around their cozy room. Three twin beds were lined up in a row, with three matching dressers on the opposite wall. The black paint on the ceiling was faded and peeling, and spiderwebs draped down from the corners. And there were books everywhere! They were stacked in neat piles on the floor, balanced on their dressers, and even spilling out from Maude's closet. CJ's stuffed bat was perched perilously atop a tower of books.

"I'll straighten this up!" Maude promised her friends.

"No worries, Maude," CJ said. "We don't mind your books. And we certainly appreciate your smarts!"

Ms. Finley smiled. "Okay, ladies, I'll leave you to your homework," she said. As she left the room, she winked at Maude. "There are far worse things than loving books!"

The next afternoon, Maude knocked three times on the enormous wooden library door. Classes were done for the day, and CJ and Tiny had gone back to their room to get a start on homework. Maude had headed for the library as soon as she could.

"Come in!" Mrs. Guttenberg called out.

Maude entered and looked around happily. It was one of her favorite rooms at the school. Overstuffed bookshelves lined every wall. Tall windows were securely covered by faded red velvet drapes. Friendly brown bats roosted in the ceiling beams. Although Boo Academy itself had electricity, the huge room was lit by hundreds of flickering candles—Mrs. Guttenberg preferred candlelight. "Just like the old, old, old days," she would tell anyone who asked.

"I hope this is an okay time, Mrs. Guttenberg," Maude said, gliding up to the librarian's crowded desk. "Once I got your note, I couldn't wait to come and talk to you. I'd love to volunteer here!"

"I'm so happy to hear that!" Mrs. Guttenberg said. "I'd love your help. As you can see, there's a lot to sort through." She swept her hand toward the many messy rolling carts of books nearby. "Do you have a little time right now?"

"Yes," Maude answered. "I'm through with classes for the day and there's still some time before the dinner gong. Please put me to work!"

And so Maude began her very first shift as a student library volunteer. It was a lot of fun! With Mrs. Guttenberg's guidance, she reshelved books, decorated a bulletin board, watered the plants, and straightened the magazine racks.

"I used to love *Wee Spirits* when I was a little girl!" she cried, holding up the magazine.

"Yes, that one's been around for many, many years." Mrs. Guttenberg looked up from her desk. "I had a subscription when I was young, too!"

Maude's favorite task was sweeping up dead flies from the windowsills and piling them on a corner of Mrs. Guttenberg's desk. They were for the brown bats in the building, the unofficial mascots of Boo Academy. Although the bats could be shy and elusive, every ghost knew that they brought good luck and successful hauntings.

"Oh, I just love the library." Maude sighed.

"Maybe you'll take over for me one day," Mrs. Guttenberg mused, smiling. "But at present, it's just about time for dinner. That's enough work for us today. Why don't you take a few moments to browse? We received a box of lovely old books yesterday. It's in the closet—I haven't even unpacked them yet."

"Thanks, Mrs. Guttenberg!" Maude agreed. They arranged for her to come back again at the same time in two days.

"Thank you for your help today!" Mrs. Guttenberg said. "And now, if you don't mind, I'll leave you alone here. I must speak to Principal Von Howl before dinner. Please shut the door when you leave."

"What about the candles?" Maude asked, looking around at the softly lit room.

"Oh, don't worry about the candles," Mrs. Guttenberg said. "When the bats swoop down for their dinner of flies, the flapping of their wings extinguishes the candles!"

"That's incredible!" Maude said.

"I've only been able to see it happen once, but it was fascinating to watch," Mrs. Guttenberg replied. "Bye, now!"

"Oooh, I'd love to see that!" Maude said. She waved good-bye as she floated eagerly toward the closet.

She pulled out the large cardboard box and plunked down beside it. She couldn't wait to see what new volumes had arrived!

The books were old and musty, and there was no better smell in the world to Maude. She was paging through an illustrated guide to goblins when the dinner gong sounded, startling her.

"Time to tidy up." She sighed to herself.

She was repacking the box when her eye

caught a small black book she'd previously overlooked.

"*A Complete Behind the Scenes Guide to Boo La La*," she mused. "Now *that* could come in handy. I'll bet there are all sorts of secrets in here!" Maude was happiest when she knew things that the other students didn't.

She debated a moment and then tucked the book into her book bag. *I'm sure Mrs. Guttenberg won't mind me taking this*, she thought. *I'll be very careful, and I'll return it on my next shift.*

All through dinner, Maude's thoughts kept returning to the small black book.

When they'd finished their homework, washed up, changed into their pajamas, and climbed into bed, Maude told CJ and Tiny about her discovery. She pulled the volume out of her book bag and showed it off.

"Just imagine what this book can tell us about Boo Academy!" she told her friends. "We can learn so much!"

"I feel like I already know enough about Boo La La." CJ laughed.

"Yeah," Tiny joined in, "I know where the dining room is, where the gym is, where to avoid Lucinda . . ."

"Oh stop, you guys!" Maude chuckled. "Maybe it's not important to you, but I can't wait to dive into it!"

The girls said goodnight, and Tiny moved around her bed until her feet were on the pillow and her head was where her feet should have been. It was the way she always slept.

As CJ and Tiny drifted off to sleep, Maude paged through the slim volume. As she'd hoped, it contained all sorts of facts and figures about Boo Academy. There were building plans, furniture inventories, sample dinner menus, lists of distinguished alumnae, and many old and yellowed photographs.

Finally, Maude closed the book, yawned, and stretched. CJ and Tiny were fast asleep. She had no idea what time it was, but she knew it was very late. As she leaned over to click off her bedside lamp, the book slid from her lap. A worn, folded piece of paper slipped out and fluttered to the floor beside her bed.

Maude sighed, tired. She picked up the paper and stuck it back into the book, then snuggled down to sleep.

Chapter Three

The dining room hummed with the sounds of breakfast. Spoons clanked in cereal bowls, girl ghosts laughed, and tiny brown bats swooped around the ceiling lights, squeaking gently. They were always welcome at Boo Academy, even in the dining hall.

"Are you okay, Maude?" Tiny asked. "I hope you don't mind me saying this, but you look so . . . messy. It's not like you!"

Maude was generally the most put-together third-grade girl ghost ever. Today, however, her hair looked like it could use a good brushing and her shirt was buttoned wrong.

"I know," Maude whispered to her friends. "I stayed up way too late last night. If you two hadn't woken me this morning, I definitely would have slept through breakfast!"

"Why did you stay up so late?" Tiny asked.

"I just couldn't put down *A Complete Behind the Scenes Guide to Boo La La*. It's fascinating!" Maude answered.

"Can I see the book again?" Tiny asked.

"Sure," Maude answered, as she eased it gently out of her bag.

"It's so old!" CJ exclaimed.

"It is very old," Maude agreed. "Just like Boo Academy. And there's so much great information inside!"

Tiny wiped her hands on a napkin, placed the book on the table in front of them, and started leafing through the pages. "Hmmm," she said. "I just see a bunch of charts and floor plans. I'm not sure what you're so excited about, Maude."

"Hey! What's that?" CJ asked, pointing at a folded piece of paper peeking out near the back of the book. "That page is not the same color as the others."

"I don't know," Maude answered, using two fingers to pluck out the paper. "It fell out last night when I was finally going to sleep. I just stuck it back in anywhere."

She smoothed out the paper on the table in front of them. It was a hand-drawn map! BOO ACADEMY was written in spidery script at the top of the page. Maude recognized a few of the school's current buildings. There was a compass rose in the lower right corner. And in the upper left corner there was an *X* drawn above the words MY TREASURE.

"What?!" Maude cried in astonishment.

"It's a treasure map!" Tiny said, her eyes wide.

"I can't believe it!" CJ said. "Where did you say you found this book, Maude?"

"It was in a box in the library closet, with a bunch of other old donated books," Maude answered. "Mrs. Guttenberg hadn't even had a chance to look through them all, but she said I could."

"Do you think it's real?" Tiny asked.

"Is there really buried treasure at Boo Academy?" CJ asked.

"Why not?" Maude answered. She picked up the book and opened the cover. "Hey, look!" she said. "It says, 'Property of A. Parition.' I wonder who that is?"

CJ and Tiny peered over at the page.

"That handwriting is the same as on the map!" CJ said. "She must have drawn—"

"Hey, what's that you're looking at?" a voice cut in. It was nosy Lucinda!

Maude quickly flipped the map over as Lucinda and Helen glided up to their table. Tiny covered it with her large hands.

"Um, it's just my Undead Language Arts paper," Tiny thought quickly. "Maude and CJ are going to help me figure out where I lost points."

"That's silly," Lucinda said disdainfully. "Why don't you just go and speak to Ms. Graves? I'm sure she could help you more than these two could!"

Maude bit her tongue. She could have told Lucinda that she had a 98 percent average in Undead Language Arts, but she just wanted her to go away.

When none of the girls answered her, Lucinda shrugged and said, "Come on, Helen. We've got better things to do."

"Good riddance," Maude said as they floated away. "That was a great excuse, Tiny!"

"Thanks," Tiny answered. "Quick thinking helps both on and off the basketball court!"

Maude and CJ grinned at her. Then Maude's face grew serious. "I can't believe we found a treasure map!" she whispered.

"I know!" CJ agreed.

"What are we going to do?" Tiny asked.

"Find the treasure, of course!" Maude answered.

"But how?" CJ asked.

"We'll follow the map!" Maude answered.

"This is so exciting!" Tiny said.

"I don't know," CJ said nervously. "I feel like we have so much going on right now. I can't think of anything but the shrieking test. I go to sleep thinking about it, I wake up thinking about it, I float to class thinking about it. I want to pass. I need to pass! I—"

"Okay," Maude said, patting CJ's hand and interrupting her nervous chatter. "I'll put the map away. Right now, our first order of business is to get you ready for the NOGS test. Tiny and I can go over shrieking techniques with you. There's really nothing to worry about. You know how hard Tiny works on her basketball game, right?"

"Yes," CJ said hesitantly.

"Well," Maude continued, "my natural talent combined with her work ethic is a surefire recipe for success!"

"You don't mind helping me?" CJ asked anxiously.

"Of course not!" Tiny answered. "We're your best friends. We stick together. Now, we've got time between classes and again at lunch. I guarantee you that Mr. Clank will be impressed with your progress by today's class!"

As they floated to Undead Language Arts, Maude explained how important breath control is to effective shrieking. Over a lunch of macaroni and cheese, carrots, and Jell-O salad, Tiny demonstrated the proper way to stand.

Finally, as they made their way up to the top-floor classroom in Coffin Hall, Maude had one last suggestion. "When I shriek, I find it helpful to picture something that makes me very angry."

"Angry?" CJ repeated.

"Yes, angry," Maude said. "It's good to get your emotions worked up a bit. Thinking about Lucinda always works for me. She's helped generate some of my best shrieks!"

"Well, I'm glad she's good for something," Tiny said, laughing.

The three friends were still giggling when Mr. Clank floated into the room, his microphone and shriek meter in hand.

"Good afternoon, girls!" he called out.

"Good afternoon, Mr. Clank," the ghost girls answered him.

"I trust you've each had a chance to do some practicing," he said. "Let's take a few minutes to warm up, shall we?"

Twelve third-grade ghosts began humming and singing, gradually growing louder and louder.

"Okay, let's hear you one at a time," Mr. Clank called. "Helen, why don't you get us started?"

"Yes, Mr. Clank," Helen said. She went to the front of the room, closed her eyes, opened her mouth, and shrieked.

The needle on Mr. Clank's meter jumped a bit, though it didn't quite reach the gray zone.

"Not bad, Helen," he told her. "Keep practicing! Now, how about you, Aminah?" Mr. Clank asked another student. "How's your practicing going?" One by one, each girl demonstrated her best shriek. Some were better than others.

When it was Maude's turn, Mr. Clank said, "I think we'll skip you today, Maude. We all know what you're capable of!" Maude ducked her head modestly, but she was beaming.

No one else came close to Maude's level, but at the very least, each ghost girl made the dial jump.

Then it was CJ's turn. She twisted her hands nervously as she floated to the front of the room. Her mind was racing as she tried to remember all the things that Maude and Tiny had told her during the day. She tried to steady her breathing as she closed her eyes and opened her mouth.

A very quiet *aaaaaiiieeeee* was all she produced. It was soft and gentle, but it was stronger than the tiny peeping she had emitted two days ago. She wasn't positive, but she thought she saw the needle give a little hop. When she looked at her classmates, she saw Lucinda and Helen rolling their eyes. But she also saw Maude and Tiny grinning at her, giving her two thumbs-up.

When she looked at Mr. Clank, she saw that he was smiling, too.

"Not bad, CJ," he told her. "You're not quite there yet, but you've made some progress. Keep up the good work!"

"Thank you, Mr. Clank," CJ said gratefully. "I'll keep practicing."

CJ's stomach was in knots. She was relieved to be a bit better today, but she still had a long way to go. Even with Maude and Tiny's help, she just wasn't sure she could get that needle into the gray zone. She didn't want to disappoint her friends and teachers. More importantly, she couldn't bear the thought of leaving Boo Academy!

"In the final few minutes before the dinner gong sounds, I'm going to go over some vocal exercises," Mr. Clank told the class. "If you practice, I assure you that you will see improvement. And we will all meet here again, the day after tomorrow."

The ghost girls dutifully began the exercises, and the air filled with shrieks and moans and wails.

Chapter Four

As soon as Maude, CJ, and Tiny got back to their dorm room after dinner, Maude closed the door. Then, she moved her desk chair under the doorknob. Now no one could get in.

"What in the world are you doing, Maude?" Tiny asked.

"Keeping anyone from bothering us. I've been waiting all day for this!" Maude exclaimed. "We need to study the treasure map!"

Maude felt in her pocket; the slim black book was still there. She'd carried it with her all day. But, just to be safe, after breakfast she'd dashed back to their room to hide the secret map.

Now CJ and Tiny watched in astonishment as she slid her hand between her mattress and the bed frame. She pulled out a small packet. It was one of her scarves, folded into a neat square around the map.

"You can't be too careful!" Maude said, smiling up at her friends.

"Whom are you hiding it from?" Tiny asked.

"Everybody!" Maude answered. "I want *us* to be the ghosts who find the treasure! I've been thinking about this a lot, and I've come up with a plan."

CJ stifled a small laugh. Maude was famous for her "plans." CJ knew that she and Tiny would go along with it, though, since Maude's plans generally worked. After all, hadn't she been able to prove, once and for all, that Ms. Finley was a ghost?

"So what are we doing?" Tiny asked.

"My plan involves us learning all we can from this map," Maude told them, "and trying to find out anything we can about A. Parition, since it seems

that it's her book and map. And, any chance we get, we'll explore the campus. That treasure is ours!"

"Careful, now you're starting to sound like Lucinda!" Tiny teased her friend.

"I'm hoping that when we find it, we'll get a special award," Maude said. There were few things that Maude liked more than awards. "Imagine how proud of us Ms. Finley will be!" she continued. "Not to mention Principal Von Howl and Mrs. Guttenberg!"

"And can you imagine Lucinda's face when we show up with treasure?!" Tiny said. "Let's take a look at that map!"

"Don't you think we should maybe ask a teacher for help?" CJ wondered.

"No way!" Maude answered. "We can do this all on our own!" She unfolded the map on her bed.

"What do you think the treasure could be?"

CJ asked, catching their excitement. "Do you think it's a chest filled with gold pieces?"

"Or maybe jewels?" Tiny suggested.

"I don't know," Maude answered. "What I do know is that someone cared enough to hide it and then draw a map."

"Do you think A. Parition hid the treasure, or just found it?" CJ asked.

"It could be either," Maude said, "but we need to investigate her."

"How?" Tiny asked.

"Did you forget that I work in the library now?" Maude asked, smiling. "You can learn anything in a library! Now let's take a look."

She turned her concentration to the map. CJ and Tiny quickly knelt beside her.

"That building is Coffin Hall, isn't it?" CJ pointed to the map.

"Yes," Tiny agreed. "I think so. Coffin Hall is the oldest dormitory at Boo Academy. But a bunch of buildings are missing from this map. Where's the gym?"

"Boo La La has probably changed a lot over the centuries," Maude speculated. "Maybe some buildings were demolished and new ones were built."

"I think that's the cemetery," Tiny said, pointing to a section on the left side of the map. "It's been here forever."

"It looks like the *X* is somewhere right in the cemetery!" Maude said. "We've got to get out there and explore."

"That's easy enough. We go to the cemetery for Haunting practice," CJ said. "But we don't want anyone to know what we're doing, right? What if Ms. Finley found out? What if Principal Von Howl sees us? I'm in enough trouble with the shrieking test coming up, and what if—"

"Okay, okay," Maude soothed her friend. "Don't worry, CJ. I promise I'll think of a way to explore secretly. I'll try to do some detective work in the library tomorrow."

"What should CJ and I do?" Tiny asked.

"Let me see what I can find out," Maude said. "You just keep helping CJ with her shrieking, okay?"

"Okay," Tiny answered.

CJ took a deep, calming breath. "Okay," she said, nodding at Maude and Tiny. "Let's do this!"

"Let's find treasure!" Tiny urged.

"Boo La La!" the girls chanted, grinning at one another.

Maude never knew where the inspiration for her plans might come from. Earlier in the school year, it was Ms. Graves, their Undead Language

Arts teacher, who had inadvertently helped Maude think of the perfect way to determine that Ms. Finley was 100 percent ghost.

Figuring out a way to get the three of them to the cemetery unsupervised seemed like a trickier task. So when the opportunity presented itself, it happened so easily that she almost missed it.

Mr. Vex, their Supernatural Science teacher, was in the middle of a lecture about moss and lichen.

"These organisms," he said, "can be immediately and dramatically affected by our energy. The presence of a ghost causes the moss or lichen to spread more rapidly."

"It's like our superpower!" Tiny laughed.

"So it is," agreed Mr. Vex. "It's an interesting haunting technique."

"What do you mean, Mr. Vex?" Maude asked.

"Have you noticed, when you've been in a cemetery, how much moss grows on tombstones?" he answered her question with a question.

"I have," Lucinda said. "But I never knew we were responsible!"

"When we spend time in cemeteries," Mr. Vex continued, "we cause moss to grow more quickly, which is not only more beautiful, but also creates a spookier place for humans. It's a win-win situation!"

"That's so cool!" CJ said.

"It is cool," Mr. Vex agreed. "And the more refined and focused your skills, the faster moss will grow. But it takes practice to release the proper amount of energy at the correct time to influence moss growth. And that's where our experiment comes in."

"I love experiments!" Maude said.

"I love moss!" CJ said.

"That's a win-win!" Tiny commented, laughing.

"I wish I could take you all out to our cemetery as a class," Mr. Vex went on. "But, unfortunately, with the NOGS test coming up, we are short on time. Instead, over the next few weeks, Ms. Finley will find convenient times for you to visit our cemetery, in small groups. You'll each be assigned a grave, which you'll visit several times."

Maude looked at CJ and Tiny with a delighted grin. She held two thumbs up. Eureka! They'd just been given a pass to get to the cemetery. CJ and Tiny grinned back knowingly. CJ's grin faded, however, when she saw Lucinda staring at them. She looked curious . . . and suspicious!

Mr. Vex continued his instructions. Each time they went to the cemetery, they were supposed to draw a picture of their assigned tombstone, paying special attention to the moss and lichen on it. Then

they'd release energy to encompass the grave. And at the end of the experiment, they were to draw a final picture.

"We'll look at all the pictures together to see the change in flora growth. The more rapid the growth, the more powerful your emanation will have been."

"My emanation is going to be the most pow-erful," Lucinda said not-so-quietly to Helen.

Maude ignored her. When class ended, she gathered up her things and started off toward the library. She had a few questions for Mrs. Guttenberg. After all, the librarian had been at Boo Academy for centuries. She might know something about the treasure!

"Wait up, Maude!" CJ called.

The three girls gathered in a tight knot in the hallway.

"We need to be really careful," CJ told her friends.

"Why?" Maude asked.

"Because I think Lucinda suspects some-thing. You should have seen the way she was watching us during the cemetery discussion." CJ answered.

"But I'm not too worried about Lucinda," Maude said loftily. "We've outsmarted her before, and we'll do it again!"

Tiny nodded.

"You know the best part about this whole map thing?" CJ whispered to her friends.

"What?" Maude asked.

"It's helped me forget all about the shrieking test!" CJ said with a smile.

"Excellent!" said Maude, as she headed to the library.

Chapter Five

"Good afternoon, Mrs. Guttenberg!" Maude called, after knocking three times on the library door. She felt in her pocket; the special book was still there.

"Hello, Maude! I'm so glad you're here," Mrs. Guttenberg answered. "Would you start organizing the reference section?"

"What happened here?" Maude cried when she spied the bookshelves. They were a mess.

"The ninth graders are studying for their emanations and auras NOGS test. I think they went through every book on the subject!" Mrs. Guttenberg answered.

"And then they just put the books back wherever they wanted," Maude said in dismay.

"It's a big reorganizing job, I know," Mrs. Guttenberg said, apologetically.

"Don't you worry, Mrs. Guttenberg," Maude said. "I'll have this mess cleaned up before the end of my shift!"

"Thanks, Maude," Mrs. Guttenberg answered. "You're a treasure!"

Treasure? Maude gulped. Mrs. Guttenberg didn't know about the map, did she? She couldn't!

As they worked quietly in the cavernous library, Maude's mind was racing. This was her chance to ask questions!

"Mrs. Guttenberg," Maude finally ventured. "Where did that new box of books you put in the closet come from?

"From a Boo alumna, I believe," Mrs. Guttenberg answered. "Did you have a chance to

look through the box? Did you find anything

interesting?"

"I did look through it—there was a cool

book about goblins," Maude answered. She con-

tinued, trying to sound casual. "Oh, and there

was a fascinating book about the history of Boo Academy."

"Well, that sounds interesting," Mrs. Guttenberg said.

"I . . . I actually borrowed the book without telling you," Maude said. "I hope that's okay. I found it after you'd already left, and I didn't think you'd mind. I'm taking very good care of it!"

"No worries, Maude!" Mrs. Guttenberg said kindly. "I'm delighted you found something interesting. Just return it whenever you're done."

"Thanks!" Maude said gratefully.

"Borrowing beautiful books is just one of the perks of working at the library!" Mrs. Guttenberg said with a smile.

Maude turned her attention to the messy reference section as Mrs. Guttenberg worked at her desk. Near the end of her shift, she came across a massive book on a bottom shelf. It was a comprehensive directory of Boo La La graduates.

"Bingo!" Maude whispered to herself. She looked at the librarian, who was smiling slightly as she read a magazine at her desk. She was paying no attention to Maude.

Quickly, Maude flipped through the pages until she came to the Ps: Paax, B.; Pable, J; Pancras, R; *Parition, A*! Maude was thrilled! A. Parition was a real ghost, and she'd been a student at Boo Academy.

Finally, Maude finished organizing the reference section.

"Is there anything else you'd like me to do, Mrs. Guttenberg?" she asked.

"That's it for today, Maude. Thanks for the great work!" Mrs. Guttenberg answered.

"Oh, Mrs. Guttenberg?" Maude hesitated at the door. "I was just wondering . . . has the cemetery always been at the back of the school, where it is now?"

"Oh, yes," Mrs. Guttenberg answered. "Our lovely cemetery has been there forever! Why do you ask?"

Maude thought quickly, but before she could come up with a reasonable explanation, Mrs. Guttenberg was speaking again. "Oh, yes—Mr. Vex told me all about your science experiment. What a wonderful way to practice energy transference!"

"Um, yes, e-e-exactly!" Maude stammered with relief.

She quickly said good-bye to Mrs. Guttenberg and headed off to the dining room. She couldn't wait to share her discoveries with

CJ and Tiny. The map's *X* was surely in the ceme-tery. And knowing that A. Parition had been an actual student at Boo made the treasure map all the more real. Who knew what it might lead them to?!

Chapter Six

The next afternoon, recess was held outside. This didn't happen often because of the sun. Even kindergarten ghosts know enough to stay inside on a sunny day! Today, however, lovely gray clouds scudded across the sky. The air was gloomy and dank. It was perfect!

After some lively gliding races, Ms. Finley joined them on the playground. She announced, "We're heading to the cemetery, girls. Ms. Graves has graciously agreed to start class a half an hour late. That will give us just about an hour to start your experiment. Ready?"

"Yes, Ms. Finley," the third grade ghost girls chorused.

"I will assign each of you a tombstone when

we get there," Ms. Finley told them. "And, Tiny, I'm going to need your expert passing-time skills. We can't keep Ms. Graves waiting!"

"No problem!" Tiny said. "Happy to help!"

It is common knowledge that most ghosts are incapable of judging the passage of time. But not Tiny—she was a whiz!

The third graders followed Ms. Finley down the stony path to the cemetery. Ms. Finley's shoes crunched, crunched, crunched on the gravel, but the students glided silently.

Soon the rusted iron gates of the burial ground were in view.

"It's so pretty!" Maude said, taking in the ancient gravestones beyond the gates. Behind the cemetery, a dark and mysterious forest, filled with huge, old trees, stretched as far as they could see.

"It's just a cemetery," Lucinda snapped as she glided past, Helen by her side.

"But it's our cemetery," CJ said, sticking up for Maude. "It's special."

"If you say so," Lucinda said, rolling her eyes. She pushed her way to the front of the line. "Where's the grave I'm supposed to work on, Ms. Finley?" she asked.

"I'll read off your names, then you'll find your assigned tombstone and start the experiment," Ms. Finley told them, handing out sketchpads. "Just let me know if you need my help finding your way. Okay, let's see . . . Lucinda, you've got Blakely Carmichael. Cheryl, you've got Sadler Snodgrass," Ms. Finley read from her list. One by one, the ghosts drifted away, sketchpads in hand, searching for their assigned tombstone in the sprawling cemetery.

Maude, CJ, and Tiny were thrilled to find that their spots were located near one another.

"I'm going to draw and then release energy quickly," Maude told them quietly, "then I'm going to do some exploring."

"Do you want me to help with your sketch?" CJ asked. She was a good artist and very quick with a pencil.

"No, thank you," Maude answered. "I'd better do the work myself."

"Do you want us to come with you?" Tiny asked.

"No," Maude decided. "I'm afraid we'll draw too much attention to ourselves if we all go. You stay and act normally."

"I'll try!" CJ said with a nervous chuckle.

Soon, the girls were lost in their sketching. The cemetery was quiet and peacefully dismal. Tiny and CJ didn't even notice when Maude put down her sketchbook, put the folded map in her pocket, and slipped away.

Though Tiny and CJ may not have noticed, Lucinda did. From some distance away, she saw Maude glide toward the back of the cemetery. She watched, through narrowed eyes, as Maude pulled a piece of paper from her pocket, unfolded it, and scanned the cemetery around her. She saw Maude turn the paper upside down and frown at it. She was puzzled when Maude turned the paper once again and shook her head.

Then Lucinda was very curious when Maude marched out of view with a determined look. Lucinda wanted to follow her but hadn't finished sketching.

Maude is up to something, Lucinda thought. Sighing, she picked up her pencil.

Ms. Finley stomped among the graves until she found Tiny, who'd finished her work for the day and was lying on the ground, staring at the gray sky above.

"How are we doing on time, Tiny?" Ms. Finley asked.

"Um." Tiny thought carefully. "It's been just about an hour."

"Thanks," Ms. Finley said, then clapped her hands several times. "Time's up, ladies!" she called. Her cheerful voice echoed around the lovely, decrepit tombstones. "Please pick up your things and meet me at the gate."

When they were all gathered, Maude gliding up last, Ms. Finley said, "I hope this time was productive for each of you. I'll make arrangements to bring you back a few more times. This is simply a fascinating experiment. I can't wait to see how the moss responds to the energy you girls bring. I know *I* love it!"

"It's been very interesting, Ms. Finley," Lucinda said, but she was looking directly at Maude.

Maude smiled at her, then turned and linked arms with CJ and Tiny.

"Did you see anything?" CJ whispered.

"Maybe," Maude answered. "But let's talk about shrieking now, and then we'll discuss the . . . other thing . . . when we get back to our room," Maude suggested.

"Ugh!" CJ said. "Shrieking again?!"

"Yes, again," Maude told her. "Tiny and I want Mr. Clank to be blown away by you today!"

"Here's hoping!" CJ said bravely, as they all headed back to the school.

Once in their room, Maude closed the door and shoved a chair under the knob.

"Again?" CJ asked.

"Again," Maude agreed.

"Did you find anything in the cemetery?" Tiny asked.

"I think I narrowed down our search area," Maude answered.

"How?" CJ asked.

"I had to wander around a little bit before I figured out which way to hold the map," Maude answered. "When I stood near the back gate of the cemetery and held the map right side up, the land-marks lined up."

"Cool!" Tiny said.

"Yes," Maude said. "Coffin Hall was right where it's supposed to be on the map."

"So you think the treasure really is in the cemetery?" CJ asked.

"I do," Maude answered. "I wanted to show you two, but then Ms. Finley announced that it was time to go in."

"We've got to get back out there!" Tiny said.

"Yes, we do," Maude agreed, with a determined look on her face.

CJ and Tiny knew what that meant. There was no stopping Maude!

Chapter Seven

"I just love Cook Eerie's rice pudding." Tiny sighed at dinner that night. She scooped up the last bit in her bowl.

"We know!" Maude and CJ chorused, laughing.

"Attention, ladies!" Principal Von Howl glided to the head of the dining room. "The NOGS tests will be held in just two days. You've all been working very hard, and I know you'll do well. Regular classes will not be held on testing day."

At that, there were cheers across the dining hall. But Maude noticed CJ looking especially pale.

Principal Von Howl continued, "Representatives from NOGS will be here to administer the tests. Twelfth graders will meet in the gymnasium for their levitation exam, ninth graders will be tested on emanations and auras in the library, and sixth graders will take their passing-through exam right here in the dining room."

"What about my third graders?" Ms. Finley asked.

"The shrieking exam will be held in the cemetery," the principal answered. "That way, the girls can work on their experiment for Mr. Vex while they wait their turn for the test."

"Wonderful!" Ms. Finley said. "There's certainly a sense of poetry in holding it in such a delightful, haunted location." She looked around at her third graders. "We're all very comfortable in the cemetery, aren't we?"

"Yes, Ms. Finley," the girls agreed.

As lunch continued, Maude saw Lucinda float up to Ms. Finley. "May I go up to my room? I'm not feeling well," she said. In Maude's opinion, she looked perfectly healthy.

"Of course, dearie," Ms. Finley answered. "Do you need someone to accompany you?"

"No, thank you," Lucinda said sweetly. "I just need to rest for a bit."

As she glided by them, Tiny saw her wink at Helen.

"What's she doing?" Tiny whispered to CJ and Maude.

"I don't know," CJ answered. "She looked fine a few minutes ago when she took the last scoop of rice pudding!"

"I don't trust her," Maude said. "But we can't worry about her. We need to get back out to the cemetery! Do either of you have any ideas for when we could go?"

"I'm sorry, but I am so preoccupied with the

shrieking test that I haven't been able to concentrate on anything else," CJ said.

Maude sighed. "I understand, CJ," she said. "And I'm sorry if *I'm* being selfish. I guess I can't concentrate on anything but the treasure map!"

"Neither one of you needs to be sorry," Tiny said wisely. "This is a stressful time for all of us. I'm just glad I don't have to tackle Ms. Finley in a basketball game again!"

That made Maude and CJ laugh.

"Remember how you bounced off her?" CJ asked.

"Remember? How could I forget?!" Tiny answered, giggling. She started reenacting the crash for her friends, to lots of laughter.

Suddenly, Maude sat up straight. "I think I have a solution," she said. She motioned CJ and Tiny closer and carefully whispered her plans.

"You're a genius, Maude!" Tiny said when she was done.

"Well, I don't know about that," Maude said modestly. "But I do think this plan will work."

The three friends chattered happily as they headed up the stairs to their room. Little did they know what was waiting for them there!

Maude opened their door and stopped abruptly. Tiny and CJ bumped into her.

"You!" Maude said.

Tiny and CJ had never heard her sound so angry.

"What's going on?" CJ asked, trying to peer around Tiny's large frame.

"What are you doing in here?" Maude demanded.

"Um—I, uh . . ." came the shaky reply.

"Who's there?" CJ asked again, desperate for a look.

Tiny moved out of the way.

"Lucinda?" CJ asked, confused. "Are we in the right room? Why are you in here?"

"Just look!" Maude said, gesturing around their dorm room. "She's been sneaking through our stuff!"

They'd caught Lucinda as she was rifling through papers on CJ's desk. Maude's stacks of books were spilled on the floor. Tiny's basketball posters had been lifted away from the wall and were each dangling by a single pushpin.

"What are you looking for?" CJ asked.

"Who cares!" Maude said, feeling in her pocket reflexively. The book was still there. She could see that Lucinda had not touched her bed.

The map was safe! "I'm going to get Ms. Finley. You're not allowed to snoop through other ghosts' rooms!"

Lucinda found her voice. "If you tell on me, Maude, then I'll . . . I'll . . ."

"You'll what?" Maude asked icily.

"I'll tell Ms. Finley that you snuck away while we were in the cemetery. When you were supposed to be working on your science experiment."

"What?!" Maude cried.

"She won't think you're such a great student then, will she?" Lucinda asked, wildly.

"You're rotten, Lucinda!" Tiny said.

"Well, Maude's not so perfect either, is she?" Lucinda retorted.

Tiny and CJ looked at Maude, who shook her head and seemed to make a decision.

"Fine, Lucinda," Maude said. "We won't say anything to Ms. Finley about this. But if we ever,

ever catch you anywhere near our stuff again, you'll be in big trouble."

"Yeah!" CJ agreed.

"Fine," Lucinda sniffed, gliding toward the door. "But I'll find out your secret, one way or another. I know you're hiding something."

Once she'd left, Maude closed the door.

"Hug huddle!" she cried, and CJ and Tiny gathered for a much needed group hug.

"We can't let her get to us," Maude said. "It's not worth it. Besides, she didn't find anything—the map is safely hidden. We'll do what we planned. After tonight, we'll just concentrate on the NOGS test and our science project. School is what's most important and I can't imagine Boo La La without CJ!"

"I know we'll find that treasure," Tiny said.

"Good things come to those who wait, right Maude?" CJ asked.

"Right!" Maude agreed.

"Boo La La!" the friends cried. And they set to work tidying up the mess Lucinda had left behind.

"I've never understood why humans are afraid of the dark," Maude announced as they floated down the path to the cemetery. The night was pitch-black and damp. A small sliver of moon was rising over the treetops, and somewhere in the distance, a wolf howled at it.

"I just love that sound!" Tiny cried.

Maude's plan had worked perfectly. They'd waited until Ms. Finley made her rounds, wishing each of her students goodnight. Then, Tiny had kept careful track of time and after only half an hour, they could hear Ms. Finley's gentle snores.

"It's now or never!" Maude had urged her friends. "Ready?"

"Ready!" CJ and Tiny answered.

"Operation Treasure Map is a go!" CJ cried as she passed through the dorm room wall, right behind her bed. Maude and Tiny could no longer see her, but they could imagine her slow and gentle descent to the ground outside. When they heard her hoot like an owl, it was Tiny's turn. She passed through the wall and immediately felt the force of CJ's levitational power. Rather than falling, she drifted slowly down to CJ's side.

"*Hoo, hoo!*" CJ called.

When Tiny looked up, she saw Maude sailing down from their second-story room, an excited smile on her face.

Now the three friends approached the cemetery gates.

"Remember, Tiny," Maude said. "Please tell us when a half hour has gone by. We don't want to push our luck!"

"Got it!" Tiny said.

Maude quietly led them to a spot near the back of the cemetery.

As they passed their science experiment tombstones, Tiny glanced at them.

"Wow!" Tiny said. "Look at CJ's grave—the moss has gone crazy!"

"It does look spooktacular, CJ," Maude agreed. "Your energy transference skills are almost as great as your levitation skills!"

CJ smiled modestly. "Thanks, you guys. I just hope my shrieking skills catch up!"

"They will, CJ!" Maude said.

They reached the far side of the cemetery and Maude turned around. Pulling the map from her pocket, she reverently opened it up and held it so that they could all see.

"I see Coffin Hall!" Tiny said.

"The *X* should be just over there," CJ said, pointing to her right. "Just where that huge tree is."

"Let's go look!" Maude cried.

The three ghost girls hurried over to the large oak tree.

As they circled around its base they poked and prodded, they lifted up fallen branches and small rocks, and they peered into the tree limbs high above their heads. CJ even levitated up, up, up, through the branches to the very tippy top of the tree.

"Nothing," she called down. "There's just a big, empty hole in the trunk up here."

"Darn it!" Maude said. "I really thought we'd find something. Come on down, CJ." .

89

"Our half hour is just about up," Tiny said, with a worried note in her voice.

"Okay," Maude said. "Let's head back to our room."

"We're not giving up, are we?" CJ asked.

"No way!" Maude cried. "I'll never give up!"

CJ and Tiny knew Maude well enough to know that they wouldn't be stopping until the treasure was theirs.

"*Boo La La!*" the friends whispered, and they headed back to their dorm.

Chapter Eight

Finally, it was NOGS examination day.

Breakfast was a very quiet meal, since so many of the students were preoccupied with the tests. Only the kindergarten ghosts seemed oblivious as they chatted and laughed.

Even Tiny seemed to just play with her food, pushing the French toast with strawberries around and around on her plate.

CJ couldn't even say out loud what was scaring her the most: What if this was her last breakfast at Boo Academy? She'd been practicing shrieking so much! Sometimes her shrieks were nice and strong, but sometimes they were practically whispers. Earlier, when she was working with Maude, she felt like her shriek had been in the gray zone. But that was just one time, with her friend. How would she fare in front of the stern NOGS officials?

A shrill whistle split the air. At the front of the room stood Mrs. Von Howl, Principal Von Howl's wife, who was also their gym teacher and lunch-room monitor. She was little and fierce and seemed to enjoy using her whistle inside even more than she did outside!

"Let's go, ladies!" she called. "Ghosts who are being tested, please head to your testing site. Everyone else, please follow me. We're going to the gym for a morning of exercise."

"I'm honestly not sure which would be worse"—CJ gave a feeble laugh—"taking the shriek-ing exam, or being with Mrs. Von Howl all morning!"

"That's the spirit, CJ!" Maude said. "You're going to do so well!"

"All right, my lovelies," Ms. Finley told her

third graders. "Please go up to your rooms and gather your science supplies, and then meet me back here. It's going to be a very busy morning!"

When they had reassembled in the dining room, Ms. Finley led the way to the cemetery. It was another beautiful day: no hint of sun and low, heavy clouds threatening rain.

"At least the weather is cooperating!" Ms. Finley said brightly as they reached the cemetery gates. "Oh! There are the NOGS officials," she said, gesturing to the left. In a corner of the cemetery were three ghosts dressed in the unmistakable NOGS uniform: gray pants, gray sweater, and gray cap. At their side, Principal Von Howl was sorting paperwork on an old table. Mr. Clank's familiar meter sat front and center.

"Okay, girls," Principal Von Howl said. "You may find your assigned tombstone and rest there.

When I call your name, please come up to the table and await instructions. Once you've shrieked, you may return to the graveyard."

He glanced down at his paperwork. "Let's get started, shall we?" he said. The NOGS officials simply stood, staring straight ahead.

"Boy, they don't look like much fun, do they?" Maude whispered as they glided to their assigned gravestones.

"Nope!" Tiny agreed.

CJ was too nervous to speak. She just shook her head.

The three friends sat down and took out their sketchbooks. This was the last day of Mr. Vex's experiment and it was time to draw their final pic-tures of the moss-covered tombstones.

One by one, their classmates were called up to shriek for the NOGS officials.

As she sat and sketched, Maude's eyes kept being drawn to the large old oak tree. She tried to stay focused on her sketch, but it wasn't easy. What was the treasure?

Then she heard her name being called.

"Guess it's my turn," she said to her friends.

"Good luck, Maude," Tiny called.

Maude was very matter-of-fact as she took her place in front of the NOGS officials. They adjusted the Shriek Meter and then signaled that she should begin. As always, her shriek sent the meter's needle jumping and spinning. The three NOGS officials looked at one another in amaze-ment, but Ms. Finley just smiled proudly.

"Well done, Maude!" Ms. Finley said. "There's no doubt about you passing, is there?"

"Thanks, Ms. Finley," Maude said, grinning.

Tiny was tested next and, while her shriek wasn't quite as powerful as Maude's, it was definitely strong enough to pass.

Soon CJ was the only third grader left. When her name was called, she stumbled to her feet. She heard Lucinda chuckle and tried to ignore her. Several feet away, Maude and Tiny were smiling and giving her two thumbs-up.

"You've got this," Tiny said.

"Remember, think of something that will make you angry," Maude called encouragingly.

As she approached the table, CJ thought, *Angry. Angry.* She heard Lucinda muttering something behind her and suddenly it was obvious. What made her mad? Lucinda made her mad! How dare she laugh at CJ? How dare she sneak into their room and look through their things? How dare she threaten Maude?

As she thought about all the mean things Lucinda had said and done, CJ could feel herself getting angrier and angrier.

When the NOGS officials finally signaled for her to shriek, CJ was furious. She stood up straight, closed her eyes, opened her mouth . . . and let out the loudest shriek she'd ever produced. The needle on the Shriek Meter swung and danced into the gray zone. One of the NOGS officials actually covered her ears. Ms. Finley was grinning hugely. CJ's shriek even echoed around the cemetery for a moment after she finally stopped.

"Impressive!" said one of the officials.

CJ felt great. She was finally starting to relax when an enormous swell of noise came from

behind her. It was a deafening sound of fluttering wings and squeaking! She turned and saw the source of the noise: an enormous cloud of brown bats rising from the old oak tree!

The students all started clapping. If one

brown bat brought good luck, seeing a whole colony was an amazing treat!

And then CJ heard what Maude was yelling: "It's the treasure, CJ!" Maude hollered. "The bats are the treasure, and you found it! Your shriek was so loud that it woke up the bats in the middle of the day!"

Maude was jumping up and down in excitement. Ms. Finley cheered in delight. Even the officials were smiling. Only Lucinda and Helen were stone-faced, glaring at Maude.

But as the immense colony of brown bats danced through the sky, all the third-grade ghost girls celebrated. The bats had certainly brought good luck; each of them had successfully passed her shrieking test!

Chapter Nine

The NOGS officials left after admiring the lovely bats.

"What a banner day!" Ms. Finley cried. "Imagine, each of you passed your exam *and* we found a colony of bats on Boo La La's grounds. It doesn't get much better than this!" Everyone cheered. Ms. Finley continued, "Come along, girls, back to school. I've got a special treat for you!"

The third graders floated back from the cemetery and crowded into Ms. Finley's cozy room.

From a shelf in her closet, she pulled a tray of snowy-white merengue cookies. "This is my secret recipe for ghost cookies," she told her students as she passed them around. "You deserve them after today's performances."

"These are wonderful, Ms. Finley," Lucinda said in her oversweet way.

"They're better than that . . . they're *boo-licious*!" CJ cried.

"What a perfect word, CJ!" Maude said.

"I'm glad you like them!" Ms. Finley said. "Now, I promised Mr. Vex that I would collect your

sketchbooks and deliver them to him this afternoon. He wants to start grading immediately."

As the girls made a pile of their sketchbooks,
Ms. Finley said, "Principal Von Howl wanted me to
let you know that you are free to do whatever
you'd like for the rest of the day."

"Boo La La!" the ghost girls shouted
with glee.

"How on earth did you do that, CJ?" Maude
asked breathlessly, once the three friends were
back in their room.

"You were awesome!" Tiny cried. "Spooktacular!"

"Thank you!" CJ smiled. "All of your advice
and practice really helped. When I went up to take
the test, I started thinking about Lucinda. I thought
about the way she can be so mean and I thought

about her being in our room without our permission. It made me so angry, I couldn't contain myself!"

"You're a genius, CJ!" Maude said.

CJ grew quiet. "I really need to thank you two. If you hadn't helped me, I'm not sure I could have passed."

"That's what friends are for," Tiny said.

"Yes," Maude agreed. "And isn't it funny that Lucinda actually helped you today, without knowing it?"

"Imagine how angry she would be if she knew!" CJ chortled.

The three friends laughed and laughed.

At dinner that evening, Principal Von Howl was pleased to announce that every single Boo

Academy student had passed her required NOGS test.

"Well done, ladies!" he said.

When he had finished speaking, Mr. Vex stood up.

"I would especially like to congratulate the third graders," he said. "They all passed a very challenging exam *and* did wonderful work on their science experiment."

From her spot at the faculty table, Ms. Finley beamed at her girls.

"One student in particular did a fabulous job," Mr. Vex continued. "I'd like to ask CJ to stand up."

Shocked, CJ looked at Maude and Tiny before standing. She could feel Lucinda's glare from across the table, but she wouldn't let it bother her.

"Not only did CJ achieve fantastic moss growth on her tombstone," Mr. Vex said, "But she artfully captured the beauty of the flora."

CJ felt herself blushing.

"Although this was not the intent of the experiment, CJ's sketches are truly beautiful. I've shared them with Mrs. Guttenberg," Mr. Vex added.

"With CJ's permission, we'd like to frame her final drawing and hang it in the library."

When he looked at her expectantly, CJ said, "I'd be honored, Mr. Vex. Thank you!"

Maude caught Mrs. Guttenberg's eye and they smiled at each other.

Then Principal Von Howl announced, "And now, let's all head to the gym for a ghoulish dance party!"

With that, the whole dining room erupted in cheers. After so many weeks of worrying about tests, they could all let off some mist!

That night, as they each lay curled in their beds, Maude, CJ, and Tiny talked about their day.

"Tiny and I are so proud of you, CJ," Maude said. "You're a first-class shrieker!"

"And an artist, too," Tiny added.

"Thank you!" said CJ. "You're the best friends a ghost girl could ask for."

After a moment, Tiny asked Maude, "Are you disappointed that the treasure wasn't a chest filled with gold?"

"No," Maude answered. "Not one bit. Having a bat colony here at Boo Academy is fantastic! Thank you, A. Parition, whoever you are!"

Maude, CJ, and Tiny drifted off to sleep with grins on their faces. Their beloved Boo La La was full of many different kinds of treasure. And they were looking forward to whatever wonderfully spooky things the next days would bring!

Don't miss the first adventure at

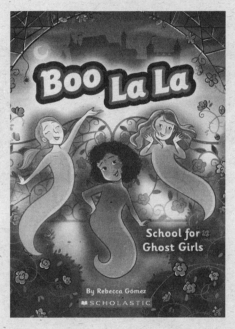

School for Ghost Girls

Maude, CJ, and Tiny are afraid their dorm mother,
Miss Finley, might be . . . human. Can the ghost girls
find out before it's too late?

Don't miss any of the
Dolphin
School
books!

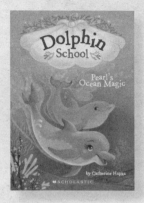

#1: Pearl's Ocean Magic

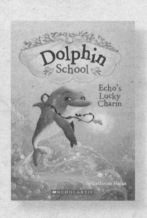

#2: Echo's Lucky Charm

#3: Splash's Secret Friend

#4: Flip's Surprise Talent

#5: Echo's New Pet

#6: Pearl's Perfect Gift

The Rescue Princesses

These are no ordinary princesses—
they're Rescue Princesses!

RAINBOW magic™

Which Magical Fairies Have You Met?

- ❏ The Rainbow Fairies
- ❏ The Weather Fairies
- ❏ The Jewel Fairies
- ❏ The Pet Fairies
- ❏ The Dance Fairies
- ❏ The Music Fairies
- ❏ The Sports Fairies
- ❏ The Party Fairies
- ❏ The Ocean Fairies
- ❏ The Night Fairies
- ❏ The Magical Animal Fairies
- ❏ The Princess Fairies
- ❏ The Superstar Fairies
- ❏ The Fashion Fairies
- ❏ The Sugar & Spice Fairies
- ❏ The Earth Fairies
- ❏ The Magical Crafts Fairies
- ❏ The Baby Animal Rescue Fairies
- ❏ The Fairy Tale Fairies
- ❏ The School Day Fairies

▣ SCHOLASTIC

HIT entertainment

Find all of your favorite fairy friends at
scholastic.com/rainbowmagic

RMFAIRY14